T0072322

Peak, Trough,
and Recovery

Peak, Trough, *and* **Recovery**

The Rhythm of Our Life

N. REVATHI VANDANA

PARTRIDGE

ISBN:	Hardcover	978-1-4828-6439-7
	Softcover	978-1-4828-6438-0
	eBook	978-1-4828-6440-3

Print information available on the last page.

To order additional copies of this book, contact
Toll Free 800 101 2657 (Singapore)
Toll Free 1 800 81 7340 (Malaysia)
orders.singapore@partridgepublishing.com

www.partridgepublishing.com/singapore

Dedication

To
The 'dear and departed': My husband and my parents
*You **knew** I could live your dream...*
My 'heart and soul': my children, Aditya and Sravani
*You **know** me better than I know myself...*
My 'furry friend on all fours': my pet dog, Ringo
*All you have ever **known** is love and loyalty...*
My 'spiritual anchor': my Guru and Guide
*Your infinite **Knowledge** is my inspiration...*
My teachers, students, colleagues, family and friends
*The **Knowing** that you are with me is a blessing...*

Let nothing disturb thee
Nothing affright thee;
All things are passing:
God never changeth;
Patient endurance
Attaineth to all things;
Who God possesseth;
In nothing is wanting;
Alone God sufficeth.

ST. TERESA
(1515-1585)
-H.W. Long Fellow (Translator)

Acknowledgements

I EXPRESS MY DEEP SENSE OF gratitude to the following people without whose help this book would not have been possible.

To my publishers Partridge Singapore for helping me to concretize my dream of writing this book.

To Dr. Rishikesh Padegaonkar, Principal, Bright Riders School, Abu Dhabi for all the encouragement and support he has given me to pursue this dream of writing.

To my son Aditya Bhushan, for his valuable suggestions and the critical evaluation of this work.

To my daughter Sravani, for her insightful suggestions regarding the theme and for her contribution in the selection of the title of this book.

To Saishree Malvi, for guiding me to my publishers.

To Shaista Khan, for helping me with the typing of the manuscript.

Preface

EVERY INDIVIDUAL SOUL COMES TO this world with his or her distinctive trajectory of life etched out by the Divine hand. This trajectory follows a pattern that is never one continuous path but rather a series of highs and lows. There may be many reasons for it but the chief reason may be that disparity, dissimilarity and diversity are all required to understand the intricacies of existence. Everything in life comes with its opposite- good versus bad, light versus darkness, joy versus sorrow and lack versus abundance. The value of one thing can only be understood by the absence of it. One can only understand the grace of a blessing when one has experienced the misery of a curse. The lack of a thing throws into sharp focus the importance of its presence in one's life. This lack or abundance of anything follows a definitive pattern in everyone's life.

Joys and sorrows are like a seesaw- joys may catapult one to the summit of euphoria but when sorrow strikes one is plummeted to the depths of despair. But that is the characteristic of life. Every inspirational book that was ever written, every wise seer who has ever spoken, all aver this same truth about life. It is also undeniable that throughout this strange journey called life we are always guided by an unseen hand that nudges, pushes, steadies, upholds and carries us, from time to time, across brambles and as well as boulders, over rocky ledges and steep inclines. Every experience that is given to an individual soul has a deeper purpose of teaching that soul to perfect itself, to pass the acid test to fulfilment. No one is spared. Yet no one is abandoned halfway. Some accomplish the journey faster and some take longer but everybody reaches the destination at some point. The chief character in this story is nothing special. She is just another soul playing the role destiny has apportioned to her, often buffeted by the winds of calamity and change but buttressed from within in the calm knowledge that ultimately good will prevail. Trials and tests are an inevitable part of life. Without them there is no growth. All people, all circumstances and all moments are motifs woven into the fabric of life and the central design emerges only on completion of the pattern. For those who believe in Infinite Wisdom the pattern becomes discernible and once this is comprehended there is no more uncertainty and fear. We realise that life is truly magical!

Life is made up of peaks and troughs but the recovery is indeed magical and miraculous. We are guided to discover our own beatitude...our own Nirvana.

Prologue

THE TIME WAS 3:30 A.M. India time. The woman took her seat by the window of the plane. The passengers were still streaming into the aisle and settling down in their seats. She gazed out of the window. The lights of the other planes were clearly visible against the darkness of the early hour. She took a deep breath to steady her nerves. She sensed a feeling of mild anxiety and took another deep breath to quell her nervousness. She looked again at the twinkling lights outside. Unexpectedly, into her mind wafted in the words of a song that she had heard so many times and grown to love. Today, the words of the song 'Airplanes' rang so true! The words, 'Can we pretend that airplanes in the night sky are like shooting stars… I can really use a wish right now…'by the American rapper B.o.B feat. Hayley Williams seemed to really manifest a miracle in her life!! The song had proved so prophetic… her wish had indeed come true. The universe had indeed answered her wish… but in what a way! She didn't know whether to revel or regret… to rejoice or grieve…what had happened was truly incredible!

As the plane got airborne the song came alive in her thoughts and a bitter sweet smile played upon her lips. Yes, it was five and a half months back that she had made that silent wish, sitting in her balcony, in the darkness of the storm ravaged city. She remembered how everything had been pitch dark and the only lights she could see were the twinkling lights of airplanes flying high up in the sky. Sitting on the cane swing, she had said out loud to the ethers -'One day I will board an international flight'. The airplanes with their twinkling lights far above the darkness that enveloped the earth as well as the sky, had indeed appeared as if they were shooting stars! She had remembered the words of the song and smiled. In the weeklong power shutdown that had followed in the wake of the severe cyclonic storm that had ravaged her city, they had suffered a tremendous shortage of power, water and essential goods and services. In one stroke nature had paralysed life and thrown everything out of focus. It was while sitting alone in the balcony and gazing out at the uninterrupted darkness all around that she had turned her attention to the twinkling stars overhead, remembered the words of the song and made that strange wish of boarding an international flight...which had so strangely been answered! Strange, because of the circumstances in which her wish had materialised. Yes, here she was, flying abroad but with the loss of her husband still fresh in her memory, still raw enough to open up the wounds of sorrow and make her heart bleed... There was much drama that she had experienced in the recent years and months and events had somehow peaked up to a crescendo but through everything that she had been forced to endure, there seemed to be an unseen hand holding her up aloft, steadying her when she tripped, even pulling her out of the deepest bogs of misfortune. This was no ordinary feeling- no – it was a conviction she felt within every nerve and cell of her being. She had suffered calamity after calamity but somehow there was always this uncanny feeling about being pulled out of every mess at the nick of time by an unseen, inexplicable presence...

She looked at her watch. Four hours left to ruminate over her past- all the events, the good and the bad that made up the designs and patterns and the flowers and the weeds that had filled the garden of her life... she had her journey ahead. She didn't know what the future held in store for her. That she had always been jinxed, of that she was sure, as sure as she was about the colour of her hair or the shape of her eyes. And this jinx had always landed her right in the middle of adventure or misadventure. But what happened now had topped it all... here she was, alone, here was Anjali Vardhan going off to an unknown place, far removed from the country of her birth with only a strong conviction in her heart about that unseen hand that she believed was her guiding light...

She closed her eyes again. Rest ...when was the last time that she had rested? Rest was a luxury that she had been denied in the last few months. Her mind travelled back to the events of the past and she decided to explore, comprehend, relive, and mull over each event that had played out the drama of her life... so much had happened in these few months, so enmeshed had her life been in a chaotic whirlpool, that until now she had not had even a moment to understand what a roller coaster her life had become. And finally, she had found that much needed respite, even if it was for a mere four hours, and she allowed her mind to enter a realm of reflection and introspection. Now she was prepared to permit her thoughts to wander as they willed, if they could at least allow her to make sense of what was happening in her life... If they could answer many puzzling questions that seemed to have no answers... the many people whose paths had crossed hers in strange unfathomable ways... the good, the bad, and the ugly- everybody who had impacted her life in one way or the other...the twists and turns her life seemed to be taking...and why fate had chosen to make her life so replete with the unexpected!

Chapter - 1

THE YEAR WAS 1987. THE month was May. She, Anjali, was the bride-full of hope, full of joy and expectation of the new world she was stepping into. Like every bride-to-be, her heart was filled with happiness, her mind was making its own resolutions about how she was going to face this new chapter of her life. The great day came, there was much rejoicing. She felt tears of gratitude for the way her parents took pains to plan and execute every detail of the wedding formalities to perfection. She remembered the look of happiness in the eyes of her mother on the day of the wedding.

"My only wish is to see you happily married," she said.

"Thank you, mummy," she replied shyly.

Her father patted her head and said, "I know my daughter will do her parents proud. It's your life now. It's up to you to make your life a blissful one. Whatever may happen you should be ready to make compromises or sacrifices because however much we may talk of women's liberation and the women of the modern world being free and being able to hold their ground, the fact remains that the future of the marriage depends largely on the woman. It is in the woman's hands to make or mar her marriage."

"Yes daddy," she had said quietly.

"I don't want to sound chauvinistic but this is my firm conviction that a woman's role in sustaining the marriage ensures a strong base for the marriage. At least that is what our marriage has taught us by experience. I fully acknowledge the contribution made by your mother to the success of our life."

He looked at her mother and she could see the look of love that passed between them. Anjali could fully understand what her father meant when he had proudly acclaimed the good qualities of her mother. She had seen the storms they had faced together in their lives. The differences of opinion, the disagreements, the debates all caused as a result of trying to appease the elders of the family, would have weakened any other relationship but not that of her parents. They had borne it all with a sense of responsibility and commitment. No storm had shaken their love for each other or their resolve to fight it out together. And many a time even if they had been right, they had had to suffer silently because of their sense of decency and propriety. Anjali was their daughter. She had seen the numerous everyday sacrifices her parents had made on many occasions and their belief in a God who throws challenges in front of his beloved children but always invests them with the capacity to tide over their difficulties ultimately.

"Yes mummy and daddy. I will never let you down." She had silently promised to herself.

The wedding had been talked about for days on end. Beginning from the wedding card that had been selected, to the gifts, the bridal trousseau, the groom's ensemble, the return gifts, the wedding venue, menu, everything had met with a general approval of the invitees and Anjali had left her home with stars in her eyes, looking forward to a very happy married life.

Her husband was quiet and reclusive, by profession a doctor, but an avid listener of western music and a voracious reader as well. Their shared interests were books and travel. Travelling to new and exotic places excited them because intrinsically they were a sensitive and artistic couple who loved nature and had a penchant for places of historical interest.

He could converse for hours together on his favourite singers, authors, artists and music albums and she marvelled at 'how one small head could contain so much information'. She would chuckle to herself remembering a line from the poem, 'The Village School Master' by Oliver Goldsmith. But she took pride in the fact that with his erudition and such a unique taste he had chosen her as his life companion. She did not underestimate herself. She was well qualified, a good artist, a good teacher and fairly good looking but she felt however, that he outshone her in his brilliance.

"I had got proposals from better looking girls but what to do, I fell for you. After all beauty is skin deep," he would often quip with a twinkle in his eyes but she could sense he was teasing her and she would retort in feigned anger, "Then why didn't you go for those better looking girls instead of going for a plain Jane like me?"

"What to do! I probably fell for that broad nose," he would reply teasingly.

"I didn't need your sympathy or charity. I could have hooked a better looking man myself," she would reply in mock anger.

This raillery would continue for some time till a more serious topic would unwittingly creep up and they fell to discussing that.

The first few years went by peacefully with each deriving pleasure from their respective jobs, he as a doctor and she as a teacher and their shared interests.

"We are in the best of professions," he said one day. "We go to bed remembering the faces of our respective clients-a grateful patient and a grateful student."

"Our contribution to society is great, isn't it?" she replied with a hint of pride in her voice. "Yes, but what about our contribution to our family lineage?" he teased her again.

She understood what he was hinting at and playfully teased him with a clever retort. "Who is always busy with his patients and his books and music? Don't blame me."

The joyful moments of those early days of togetherness were etched forever in her heart. Other sweet memories crowded into her mind... The innumerable scooter rides to movie halls thirty kilometres away, the lone rides back home in the dead of the night after a second show movie, the cooking sessions of experimentation with exotic cuisines, the countless cups of coffee they downed by competition, their animated discussions on a wide range of subjects, listening to the Beatles or Beethowen on rainy evenings, browsing in used book stalls for hours and the thrill of buying a classic for a paltry fifteen rupees- this was their life, filled with simple joys and sweet pastimes.

Chapter - 2

ANJALI ALSO REMEMBERED HOW HELPING people in need was a passion she and her husband shared. One only needed to ask for help, whether it was material, monetary, or otherwise and they would be ready to extend help in any way they could.

This passion for helping people made Anjali play the part of a mediator for a few of her relatives also. She and her husband had successfully helped to clinch marriage deals for two of her cousins. Whether it was match making or helping relatives by arranging for operations or treatments or rendering any other kind of help they would not hesitate even for a second. It was as if the Samaritan instinct was in their very blood. Both were goaded by an altruistic love of humanity and believed in the 'do-good' 'feel-good' factor.

"If by assisting people in some way or the other we can bring cheer into somebody's life, it's worth doing it, isn't it?" Anjali would ask her husband.

"Agree," he would reply, 'I do not know whether God keeps accounts or not but you will certainly figure on the top of the list of his favourites.'

He would grin disarmingly and she would be glowing with happiness.

This very attitude of the couple made them cheerfully take up the responsibility of helping their relatives even during childbirths. Being a doctor he volunteered to make arrangements for the delivery in the hospital where he worked and she cheerfully helped the expectant mother during and after the birth of the child.

Being inexperienced was in no way a deterrent to understand an infant's behaviour. Lovingly and with the expertise that comes naturally and instinctively to a woman, Anjali would hold the infant in her arms and rock the baby to sleep.

'I wonder when I would have my own to hold in my arms and marvel at the magic I have created …for a birth *indeed* is magic… and the joy of creation is an experience totally unique and the exclusive prerogative of a woman,' she mused silently. When you desire something very much and you are at the point of getting it but by a mischance it slips off your fingers! What do you do? … You began to flail your arms about … grope…try to hold it desperately …… and finally realise you've lost it! The pain that follows the loss is maddening, in comprehensible, and leaves you completely shaken. Anjali had to undergo all that when she miscarried her first pregnancy in the first trimester. How she had wanted the baby! How she had ached for one! How she had longed to have her own child when she had helped others to have theirs…

Why? God! Why? She cried inconsolably. What had she done to deserve such a heartache? She had conceived after four years of marriage and when it was finally confirmed that she was indeed with child her joy had known no bounds. And now this! One innocent journey by a rickety bus and it had cost her dearly. She lost her baby!! She had torn her hair and wept bitterly but could not fathom why God should have denied her the very thing she longed to have. Four years of endless waiting and anxiety and now this!

"Don't cry. There is a time for everything. Till the right time comes all your crying will not help. Your children will come but at the God ordained hour." These words, spoken by a wise aunt made her come to terms with her predicament and she decided to pray sincerely from that day onwards.

In her desperation she had started consulting astrologers, palmists, tarot card readers and the like. Finally a colleague who had an uncanny gift of face reading had predicted, 'You will conceive in the second half of this year. Your son will be born next year in summer when the mango season is in full bloom.' Her heart sang with joy. She was willing to believe anything. "I am not a sceptic and I won't doubt his words," she said to her husband resolutely.

"I wish I could be as sure as you are," her husband sounded worried.

"No, no negativity please," she implored. "It is said in the Bible that faith can move mountains. I believe my friend's words. He had predicted to another friend of mine, when she enquired about her future husband that he would come from the high seas. And exactly as he had predicted, a Naval officer came into her life. They fell in love and got married. And he says all this by merely reading one's fate on one's face." She seemed to be defending the veracity of her statement.

"Fine. Let's hope for the best," he replied with a smile.

Her devout prayers continued unceasingly inspite of the assurance given by her friend about the certainty of the arrival of her bundle-of-joy by the summer of the following year. With amazing precision the prediction came true. She conceived by September and in the summer of the following year, she was blessed with a healthy male child. She told the story of her amazing experience to one and all. If people still doubted her she gave no thought to it. The miraculous had indeed occurred in her life and she was grateful to God for his munificence and to her friend whose amazing prophecy had worked such a magic in her life!

But this experience also left her wondering about the mystery that was life. There was so much to know, so much to comprehend, so much to explore. For a minute she imagined the macrocosm that was the universe and the speck that she herself was in that large scheme of things The whole amazing phenomenon of the birth of her child exactly as predicted by her face- reader friend, led her to conclude that there was so much mystery in life and beyond life and so little did people understand it! Half of our lives are spent in clamouring for material comforts and mundane objects and we don't understand that there is a more real world that is waiting to be explored… that is the realm of the Spirit. On and off such contemplation of the esoteric kind would unwittingly creep into her thoughts and she would find her mind drifting… Her reveries were broken into by the cries of her infant son and she pushed aside those thoughts to a later day, content now to immerse herself in the joy of bringing up her infant son.

She lived the role of a mother to perfection. Her greatest wish had been fulfilled! She remembered the words of her aunt "...at the God appointed hour." How right she had been. No point rushing. In fact no pressurising at all. All we have to do is to make a wish and release it to the ethers. Someday... at some God chosen hour... the wish will come back to be realised in our life.

The universe is prepared to give... all we need to do is trust and wait. She had experienced the inexplicable many a time before, but the birth of her son and the amazing manner in which the prediction had been fulfilled reaffirmed her faith in the Infinite power of the Universe.

Life indeed is a marvel. She could understand what the great William Shakespeare had meant when he said- 'there are more things in heaven and earth than are dreamt of...'

Chapter - 3

HER SON WAS A GIFT indeed from the heavens and she put her heart and soul into fulfilling her role of mother to perfection. Be it any age, children held a fascination for her. Now that she had her own flesh and blood in her hands she thought herself lucky and truly blessed to have experienced this joy of being a mother.

This love for children had also helped her to become an instant hit with children. This passion for children was in fact one of the reasons for her choosing to become a teacher by profession. The thought of children brought on the memory of dear faces that she had grown to love over the years. In every face was reflected the countenance of God. God was everywhere- not only in nature, in the flowers, fruits, trees, leaves, hills, valleys and streams but also in the innocent face of every child. Anjali also believed in past lives. She was sure that her deep love for children had to do with some fact of her past life. It is believed that our present lives have a purpose which is connected to our past lives. We are either atoning for past mistakes or reaping the fruits of past good deeds. Whatever it was, though she didn't know how her own past life could have impacted her present life, she was sure of one thing. Her soul was indeed connected to the love of children in a very special way. She wouldn't waste this God given opportunity but do all she could for children. And with this intention she had thrown herself heart and soul to the job of teaching and mentoring all those children whose paths had crossed hers. She had scores of young fans and she received love from them enough to last not one, but many life times. Added to that special feeling for children, was her deep passion for her subject. She loved her subject –English. She sensed that this passion for the subject literally ran in her blood- her father, her mother, her brother all had somehow had that common love for English and she had heard of ancestors who had been poets and writers. She concluded that since this passion could be traced back to her ancestors, it was no wonder that she had such an intense love for it. She revelled in poetry- the Romantic poets were her favourite. She had the deepest reverence for their poetry.

Lines of Tintern Abbey could send her into a rapture!! Like Wordsworth, she could sense the 'Spirit' of nature and be chastened by it… the beautiful imagery of Keats' poems, the bizarre and mysterious world of Coleridge's imagination… They were not only poets but seers who could peer into the realm of the divine… such was their gift!

Chapter - 4

Anjali's thoughts then wandered off to her children. She had left behind in India, what was now *left* of her family- her son Neel, her daughter Nitya and Reggie their five year old male Labrador. Such a beautiful family. Such lovely children... she remembered the tall handsome Neel with his many talents- brilliant at maths, an agile hip hop dancer, and an expert football and basketball player. Nitya, with her 'milk and roses' complexion, as her husband used to describe her, was the darling of the family. Like her father she had inherited a taste for music and an active mind that would always ask questions and come up with ready wit that would enliven any party. Anjali remembered their childhood times. How annoying Neel used to be when she had to pin him down to evening study time. How she would run around with a ladle in hand, threatening to thrash him! Only then would he submit to her will! Nitya had always been pliant and sweet. No rebellious behaviour, no tantrums. She thanked God for their lovely natures. It was unfair that at such a young age they were being put to such trials.

When Anjali's father had passed away, Nitya had been heartbroken. "He had promised to be alive till I got married. Now, he has gone. He has cheated me," she had said sobbing inconsolably. And yet the same seven- year- old had consoled her bereaved grandmother with words that reflected a wisdom that far belied her age.

"Stop crying grandma! It was God's will that grandfather should go before you. He was so ill. If he had remained alive he would have suffered so much. Would you have liked to see him suffer? Be happy that he is with God. Do not cry. If you cry, he will not be happy. His soul would not be at peace."

Those words of wisdom coming from the innocent lips of a seven year old child! Anjali had wondered at the maturity the child had displayed. Years later, Nitya admitted that she herself did not know how she could have spoken words of such depth.

"Either it was grandpa speaking through me, or maybe God conveyed this message through me to console grandma," Nitya had surmised.

But this wisdom was not a momentary thing. Anjali knew that both the children had sagacity and an understanding of life that was surely a gift of God. Noble natures were rare. But in being blessed with such children she had been twice blessed indeed. The most recent storm that had ravaged their lives, also gave proof of the steadiness of her children. They were the anchors to which her life was now moored and a sacrifice on their part, immeasurable by any standard, was what had got her on this plane... They had been there, standing by her, supporting her and even taking charge when she had been overwhelmed by moments of grief and she was prepared to do anything to give them a good life...

And she was also grateful to little Reggie who, with his liquid brown eyes, soulful looks, and cute antics, had the whole family eating out of its paws! Now Anjali understood God's plan and strategy. She had often wondered why she had allowed herself to agree to her children's demand for having a pet and that too a Labrador! In their two bedroomed flat it had really been a challenge, trying to house a dog as well!

But now she understood why Reggie had come into their lives. The manner in which their lives had somersaulted, if it had not been for the presence of Reggie she actually couldn't have expected her children to cope with the bereavement alone. She was now sure that the decision to leave her children back in India and go abroad to work, had been a good one. With Reggie around, one couldn't be depressed. This little furry champ was a sure antidote to any sort of gloom. And they were bound to be safer with Reggie guarding them in the house, what with its regal lion -like looks!

How she longed to snuggle up close to its soft furry coat and hold its dear face with the prominent, watery snout, in her hands and feel its soft tongue as it licked her cheeks...For a moment the memory of all three- her children and the little dog living bravely by themselves, made her eyes well up with tears. God's purpose was hard to understand. One had to be still and wait for his plan to unfold... Never had Anjali felt more unsure of their future as now...And yet there was this tugging in her heart that told her to cling to God's hand even through the tunnel of darkness that they were traversing...

Chapter - 5

J YOTI...THE NAME CREPT IN UNEXPECTEDLY into her mind. Three years had passed... three years since the death of that young girl who, like a Shakespearean heroine, had been a tragedy queen and whose tragic flaw had been her inordinate temper. She remembered Jyoti when she had first walked into her house offering her services as a nanny for Anjali's second child, little Nitya. Jyoti had only studied upto class 5. But she more than made up for her lack of education with her great presence of mind and intelligence. Soon she became a favourite of all. She was smart, adept at cooking, and even at fixing little mechanical or electrical defects in the household gadgets. Anjali was amazed- Jyoti barely had any education but with an agile mind she could perform any task effortlessly. Anjali tried to persuade her to return to school and complete her education. She even offered to teach her at home. But Jyoti had a stubborn belief that formal education was just not her cup of tea.

"Amma, my head just cannot take in any information from books. I am not at all comfortable with the printed word." She would reply adamantly.

"You have just developed a fear of reading and writing. With some help you can easily overcome this fear. You should try to educate yourself. Then you can get a better job." Anjali tried to explain to her.

But her answer had been a stubborn 'no'. Ultimately, Anjali gave up all attempts to try to persuade her to change her mind.

Anjali remembered how with the passage of time Jyoti had grown up to be more and more adamant and ill tempered. This ungovernable temper made her more and more unpopular amidst her kith and kin. In Anjali's family also resentment against her started brewing. The complaints by her children against her behaviour started increasing day by day. The girl had excellent qualities but her one tragic flaw was the stubborn streak which became worse as she grew older.

"Something must have upset her," Anjali's husband tried to explain in her defence, because he was also fond of Jyoti.

"But why is she being so unreasonable?" Anjali demanded agitatedly. "She doesn't confide in me in spite of my attempt to understand and help her."

"Is it because of a failed love affair? After all she is eighteen now. Quite capable of getting involved in love affairs." Anand looked at her questioningly.

"That is the whole problem. She doesn't reveal anything to me. And to think I was substituting for her mother!" she smiled wryly.

"Why blame yourself? You did your best. If she doesn't wish to disclose her secrets to you, you cannot help it. But I guess frustration is the chief cause for this sort of behaviour."

"Whatever may be the reason," Anjali interrupted him, "Her temper tantrums are unbearable. Even the kids are objecting to it."

'Hmm…' was all Anand managed to say and fell silent.

It came as no surprise to Anjali when one fine day Jyoti came to her and announced her intention to quit working in her house.

"But my dear, isn't it too sudden?" Anjali asked as her mind raced to comprehend what Jyoti was telling her. The very boat of her life seemed to rock… it meant many things… Looking out for a new help… training her up once again… The years Jyoti had spent in their house which made her develop affection for the child. Anjali remembered how she had shown so much understanding towards this girl, even pampering her to the extent that her relatives had even chided her for being so lenient towards a mere house maid! But Anjali had put up with it all because of her nature that made her treat Jyoti as she would treat any other child.

"I am leaving for Hyderabad, madam. I have found work with better pay." Jyoti spoke in her usual taciturn way which had been her behaviour of late.

'Oh!' was all that Anjali could manage in the beginning. Then, after a moment's silence she asked her, "Why do you want to leave? After spending all these years with us? Are you sure you are taking the right decision? We are concerned about your safety."

"I am very sure madam. I will be paid Rs. 5000 for full time work and of course food and lodging is free. The lady who is taking me is not unknown to you. She is your student's mother. Remember that lady who had invited you to lunch at her house to celebrate her son's success in the class ten Board examinations? The boy's name is Amit. They have got transferred to Hyderabad and since her husband will be away on business trips and even her son will join a hostel she wants me to stay with her on a full time basis. I am not having much growth here and I have family responsibilities so I have decided to leave," she said with a note of finality in her voice.

Anjali knew better than to argue or reason with her. She knew how stubborn Jyoti could become when contradicted. She acquiesced with just a succinct, "When are you leaving?" "A month from now", Jyoti replied, "to help you look for a replacement."

After that, time had just flown. A replacement had been found, Jyoti left for Hyderabad and it was two years before she had heard from her again.

Anjali had often longed to hear what became of the girl who she had sheltered in her house for so many years and who had been almost a part of her family. She couldn't comprehend the cold manner in which Jyoti had broken all ties and moved on in search of greener pastures. Even her husband Anand had indulged her as if she were his own child. What Anjali and Anand could understand and appreciate was the high degree of integrity the girl possessed. She had been loyal, hardworking, and never resorted to petty thievery.

"Her behaviour baffles me," Anand said one day. "If it was marriage she was on the look- out for, we could have tried to search for a suitable groom." But the abrupt manner in which she left us surprises me. I hope she is safe…"

"I was also concerned about her safety but would she listen? One can't reason with adamant people," said Anjali with a note of helplessness in her voice. After two years of complete silence Jyoti had shown up on their doorstep again looking older than her twenty years, and appearing thin and emaciated.

Her pride came in the way of her divulging any truth about the happenings at Hyderabad, but Anjali could guess that she was not happy. "I quit work there because the weather in Hyderabad didn't suit me," she said and Anjali could sense a note of reluctance in her voice to talk anything more on the subject. Anjali decided not to press her for more information if she was disinclined to talk about it. "I came to see you, doctor babu and the children," she said. "I will be working somewhere in this city only." She added.

Subsequently they saw very less of her till one day her own maid brought the news that Jyoti was very ill and her condition was quite serious. Anjali was shocked. She found out the address where the girl lived and paid her a visit. One look at the girl's swollen body told her that there was probably no hope left for her. On enquiry she found out that she had been suffering for months and had been in and out of some hospital in her village. Why they hadn't got her treated in any hospital in the city was a mystery. Anjali asked to see the medical reports but the family clearly weren't interested in the help she was trying to extend. It was all very mysterious but whatever their reasons for this silence, her heart brimmed with pity for the poor girl who was so terribly close to death. She could read the look of helplessness, regret, sadness and despair in those pale eyes. The eyes had already taken on a grey colour with life ebbing out of them by the second.

Two days after her visit she received the news of Jyoti's death and with her death came all sorts of rumours… That she had contracted some disease due to an illicit affair! Anjali was not interested to know any details. She saw the death of the girl as an example of a life gone waste, an intelligent girl who would have made a perfect wife for anybody… now gone for ever… all because of that stubborn streak that had made her leave the security of her home to go on an almost freakish pursuit of a quixotic dream…and walked into a snare that had cost her, her very life. Karma… that was it… Everything boils down to it. No one can escape it. Sooner or later all accounts get settled, all dues paid… God gives us the free will to choose… but very often our judgements get clouded by our own ego… That prevents us from seeing the obvious… added to that is our own 'Karma' acquired over previous lifetimes which pursues us till the debt is paid.

Whatever it was, the whole family mourned the loss of this young life. Her son, Neel wore a grim look but Nitya her daughter wept for Jyoti who besides being her nanny, had been her playmate too when Anjali had been busy with her duties as a teacher and looking after Neel's studies in his Kindergarten years.

For Anjali and Anand too, it was a sad loss. Jyoti had been with them for eight long years. She had been barely twelve when she had started working in their house and they had such happy memories of the girl who had won their hearts with her intelligence, presence of mind, and honesty. It was inexplicable why life should have dealt her such a raw deal.

Chapter - 6

'Karma' ...yes karma had also given Anjali good friends. Friends who had stood by her through thick and thin... friends who had been there when she had needed a shoulder to cry on or a heart to unburden to. There were Shreya, Geeta and Esha in whose company she had spent many a joyous hour. There were plenty of outings they had gone on, some wonderful journeys undertaken as part of teacher training workshops at New Delhi and quite a few local picnics and shopping trips, not to mention private get- togethers, complete with dinners, music and dancing.

Anjali remembered with nostalgia the year end parties they used to have at Geeta's place, the men retreating to the cozy comfort of the drawing room and indulging in the typical men's conversations, a glass in each hand and the woman busy in the kitchen getting ready for the midnight hour feasting and the children busy with their own games. Then would be played the music and the sprightly, chic Esha would begin coaxing everyone to come and join her for a dance.

"What is a party without dancing, folks?" She would insist and soon with her skills at persuasion she would get everybody on the dance floor of Geeta's drawing room, dancing enthusiastically to the popular numbers of the day.

Surprisingly, it was the children who would show reluctance to join in. Especially the boys... the mothers had to literally pull them to join in.

"Neel! don't be a spoil sport!" Anjali remembered, how she had to admonish her son for refusing to dance.

"Mummy, you know how well I dance. I love dancing but with you, daddy, uncles and aunties dancing around I feel so embarrassed."

"But it is the night of the thirty-first dear. Tonight it is okay for everyone to dance." Anjali would explain and get him to agree.

This supposed reluctance would only last for a short time and soon the thirty first night fever would 'catch on' and everybody young and old would be waltzing around in tune with the music. At the stroke of the midnight hour the New Year was ushered in amidst more dancing, cutting of a cake and merry feasting.

Anjali remembered how everybody used to enjoy the food she had prepared, under the direction of the chef, Anand, whose fertile mind could cook up new ideas for exotic recipes that turned out to be instant hits!

She also missed the exchange of witty repartee and the poetry reciting sessions… Sheena quoting her favourite lines from Ghalib, the Urdu and Persian language poet, Dr. Ranjit with his impeccable wit and flawless narration of jokes, Shreya a captivating beauty with her infectious laughter which made any party sizzle with zest, Geeta with her capacity to make others go into peals of laughter with her humorous everyday anecdotes and Esha whose exuberant spirit would galvanise everyone into that partying mood…

But life is not all 'sugar and spice and all things nice.' She recollected how each of their families had its own share of fortunes and misfortunes. Each of her friends had also seen it all- depressions, misunderstandings with spouses, estrangement, suspicion, anxiety, trouble with adolescent children, family problems, sickness… the list was endless and yet troubles come and trouble go… nothing stops…nothing ever stops… not for her or for anyone…life is meant to happen…to continue in spite of obstacles…like a river that keeps flowing …like the brook that keeps flowing… Singing its endless song of immortality, 'For men may come and men may go but I go on forever.'

Anjali smiled –How natural for these beautiful lines to pop up in her mind. Tennyson to her rescue…she smiled again. We think so much, reflect so much, analyse deeply, recollect, dissect, apply logic, apply wisdom, wit, whatever…and for what? What are we… but ripples in the ocean of existence. Why don't we just 'be' and not fidget so much. Why don't we just keep quiet so that we can truly understand ourselves?. 'Pablo Neruda' Anjali smiled again. Poetry is indeed a blessing… those words are so full of wisdom… poets are indeed prophets… they are given that light of understanding and perception which sets them apart from others… she came back to her thinking about her friends. Her friends- Anjali smiled recollecting each of their dear faces. She remembered with special fondness her friend Shreya, who was her twin self in terms of shared interests, passion for English Literature, love for children and love for teaching. The duo had even earned the titles of 'Shakespeare' and 'Wordsworth' for their deep interest in literature of a kind. They complemented each other. A poem or a prose piece or a theme for a play… whatever it was, they created together…One began it and the other concluded it…that perfectly attuned were their minds. 'Megha' another friend, whose beautiful combination of wit and wisdom was a source of inspiration for her. Megha was a few years younger than her and still displayed such a maturity and understanding of human nature that Anjali often counted herself lucky to have found such good friends. And there were also all her dear school mates whom she had given up as lost forever when they had parted ways after their schooling days but with whom she had connected again, thanks to technology. She remembered the years of longing to run into them on some journey or some tourist spot or during the school workshops she had attended in various cities. Every journey would start with an earnest prayer to God… 'Please God …let me meet any old classmate…' only to come up with no success! For almost two decades that wish had remained unfulfilled … As if God had turned a deaf ear to all her entreaties. And yet out of the blue the wish had got answered when her daughter got her introduced to one of the social media sites and all at once she had connected with not one but dozens of her school mates! Seema, Meera, Malini, Vinita, Uma, Rajini,

Shobha, Archita... And it appeared as if all her friends had been similarly bit by the same bug and had wanted to connect back with one another. The most amazing aspect was that Anjali got connected with her 'lost' childhood friends just a month before the first reunion of her batch mates at her school!

This was what could be called Divine Providence. For all the years of apparent silence by God, it wasn't that he was not listening. He was just waiting for that opportune time when she would be able to realise his great gift! The warm hugs and kisses, the exchange of information spanning a time frame of three decades, the laughter, the merry making and the feasting could not be expressed in words...the joy had to be experienced to be believed! The waiting had made the moment all the more sweet... Amazingly the bonds had held firm and they connected easily and warmly as if they had parted only the day before. Parted at fifteen and yet the bonds of love had held firm! Time could deal no blow to the childhood memories and love that they had for each other and age was no matter – they had become fifteen year olds again... rollicking with mirth and laughter.

And the bonanza was to be able to meet not only her friends but some of her beloved teachers who had attended the reunion celebration! The teachers who had been a vital part of Anjali's growing years...the teachers who had kindled the fires of learning in her heart and had been her joy and inspiration. Could she ever thank God enough?

She smiled as she remembered the words of her husband when she had returned from the reunion looking ten years younger.

"I would thank technology for enabling such a thing to happen," he said smiling indulgently at her.

"Yes technology and God as well. For it is he who created man and gave him the intelligence to come up with technology," she would declare in defence of God.

"Okay, have it your way," he would laugh, agreeing with her.

Midstream...

"**M**a'am what would you like to have? Veg or Non Veg meals?" The voice of the airhostess interrupted her reveries. Anjali opened her eyes and spelt out her order. The airhostess handed over the breakfast tray to her.

"Coffee, tea or juice ma'am?"

"Coffee,", she replied instantly. Nothing like good aromatic coffee. The early morning hour, with the night sky still aglow with the twinkling stars, seemed just the right moment to savour hot coffee.

Anjali sipped slowly, downing the hot coffee in slow, eager gulps. The warm beverage coursing down her throat gave her a good feeling. She felt instantly better once the breakfast was completed and the empty cartons had been collected. Anjali snuggled herself into a comfortable position intending to catch a little sleep. But sleep eluded her. She shifted several times to get into a more comfortable position but just couldn't seem to fall asleep. She realised she had ruffled up too many ghosts of past memories and involuntarily the thinking returned. Her mind raced back to her reminiscing and before she knew she was already back into her world of reveries. She struggled to empty her mind of all thought and just live for the present. The reality of the present moment was that she was off to a new start... but too much had happened in her life and to disentangle herself from the past events was near to impossible. She resigned herself to her thinking, as memories crowded into her consciousness...

Chapter - 7

IN EVERY SOUL'S JOURNEY THERE is a testing period when it has to pass through the severest of trials and tribulations. Anjali was no different from any other person similarly facing such a predicament. But in her case it was as if she was the chosen child of fate to undergo its most complicated machinations. And especially when one finds oneself in the very core of trouble… in the very eye of the storm, one loses all sense of perspective. I t is very like being tossed and rolled in mid ocean with no hope of ever being rescued. For Anjali the trouble germinated at home, almost alongside the good that was happening in her life.

On one side life seemed to be loading her with gifts- the birth of her children- her precious two, who were an answer to her deepest desire to experience the joys of motherhood. On the other hand was her husband's insidious dependence on alcohol which was casting ominous shadows on the happiness of their household. Caught up in the vortex of daily chores, of looking after two young children and managing her own job at school, Anjali did not notice that the habit of drinking nightly was assuming alarming proportions.

She accosted him one day, determined to somehow make him see the bare truth that he seemed not to see or was pretending not to.

"What is wrong with you? Why are you bent upon ruining our happiness? Please understand. The kids are so small. We have responsibilities. Please give up this habit. Children are scared of you when you drink and your smoking will turn us all into passive smokers. Do something. Please give up or at least make an attempt to reduce this habit gradually."

His answer would be, "Hey! don't be scared. I am not a hard core alcoholic. Just one nightly dose to help me sleep well. That's all. No worries please!"

That was it. Just that simple an answer… Just a wriggling out from an unpleasant situation with a frivolous reply. In spite of all his assurances she had her own doubts and she knew she had every reason to fear the worst! Addiction was a canker that would eat into his core, destroy his health and ruin her family. She continued hounding him, counselling him, pleading with him and even having verbal battles! The problem was the way her husband reacted to all her tirades- he wouldn't lose his temper- all he did was give her assurance that it was not a great problem and that he could easily give it up whenever he wanted to. But that was the hitch. It didn't look like he intended to give it up at all.

If at all, the problem only worsened with every passing day. Each day that passed even seemed to change his behaviour. When he was sober he was his calm, sweet self. But when he was high on alcohol, he was a different person. His demeanour would change, the tone of his voice would change, a furtive look would hover in his eyes… his essential goodness would prevent him from resorting to physical violence. Still, the changed behaviour, the tone of sarcasm, the slightly demented look, whenever he was 'high' on alcohol would be intolerable to her and cause her to burst into tears.

"Aren't you realizing that you are hurting me?" She would shout in anger at him. "How do you expect me to live with you when you behave like a split personality… It's like living with two persons at the same time. Please understand. Even I am working! Even I need peace and quiet and a happy atmosphere at home. Your being so irresponsible is really so unfair. I deserve better than this! For reasons only known to him, God himself seemed to be silent and distant. Why was he allowing this to happen to her? She could see her happiness being marred for no fault of hers. Still in her early thirties and with a long life lying ahead of her she wondered how she could manage to keep the boat her life afloat without foundering…without drifting away to an unknown future… without running aground on some rocky shore…

But life has a capacity to repair and restore. Inspite of the nightmare of facing a husband who persisted in his nightly routine of drinking, Anjali with her capacity to bounce back from any calamity, learnt to cope with his habit, drawing some consolation from the fact that at least he did not have any other vices like gambling or flirting. And there was never any physical violence involved in his behaviour towards her…a perfect gentleman even then…she smiled to herself at the irony of the situation. When one is faced with difficult choices one learns to go for the better of the two. She had the choice of either adjusting to his routine or take a more bolder step and try to live independently with her children. She dismissed the second option almost as soon as it presented itself, because she couldn't imagine ever taking such a drastic recourse. Her love for him and the knowledge that he too loved her, inspite of his inherent weakness for the booze, made her drop that option altogether. And wasn't he such a fine person otherwise, and what about their shared interests- their mutual love of books, music, films, travelling…they at least provided a sound basis for a good companionship. And more than that, she had the children to consider. She decided that she would never make them face the trauma of a broken home. She had often read that highly intelligent people were a little weird… and usually difficult to live with. The same was the problem with her husband. She also knew that one could not possibly have all the blessings. Whatever happiness was being denied to her in the form of marital bliss was being more than compensated for in the form of her precious children. They were the kind any mother would be proud to have. She couldn't ask for anything better so she decided to live with whatever fate had written for her and tried to make a 'lemonade' out of the mere 'lemons' that life was apportioning out to her.

A suggestion from her friend made her ask her husband one day, "Why don't you join a de-addiction camp?"

She knew the answer even before he could voice it- "My problem is not so acute. I can exercise control," was all he would say, adamantly, putting an end to all argument. What she could not fathom was how he could be like this and allow his habit to ruin his health. The biggest irony was that being a doctor he could be so blind to his own weakness.

Anjali had no option but to resign herself to her predicament. No one can predict the future... So let the future take care of itself... 'I will live in the *now*... try to hold on to the present moments of happiness... inhale the fragrance of the flowers in my garden and ignore the weeds... understand that one cannot have the best of everything. If this is my lot, I will accept it and fight every challenge with every ounce of strength I have.' She resolved, believing with all her sense of faith that God would not forsake her. Theirs was a good family. Both were in professions that made them serve humanity-he, his patients... she, her students. This little contribution to the world on their part, should insure them against any winds of adversity, should ensure them of God's protection. And with these thoughts, Anjali forged ahead shedding silent tears within the four walls of her bedroom, but smiling broadly to the world outside, so that none was aware of the daily challenges she braved, but only saw the ever smiling, blithe spirit that she was, loved by all and especially her students for whom she was teacher, mother, friend and mentor- all rolled into one. She found her greatest happiness in the company of her students and by living the role of a teacher to perfection.

Once she was in the class facing her students, all her troubles would take a back seat. So lost would she be to all else that it was only when she would be driving back home, that the dread of facing another of the stormy scenes would begin to haunt her with a sense of foreboding and disquiet. She would try to avoid confronting her husband just to ensure that the tranquillity of her home could be maintained. But she also realized that by keeping quiet she was sending out the wrong signals...that she was getting reconciled to his way of living. Yet, the peace of the house was of paramount importance to her and she resolved to avoid ugly scenes as long as she could and till she reached the end of her tether. Anand also seemed to sense the disharmony that hung like a pall of gloom in their home but though at times he tried to reduce the frequency of the drinking he didn't make much effort to entirely rid himself of the scourge.

So the peace that prevailed in the house was like a thin veil that could be torn asunder any moment. But children have a way of brightening the dullest days. For both Anjali and Anand the kids were the gates that kept the deluge of misery in check. Their studies, their games, outings with them, birthday parties, shopping sprees, buying Barbie dolls or G.I Joes, dishing out delicacies for their various tastes kept the household busy through most of their years of schooling. When a storm or two did become inevitable, Anjali merely began to face it like a passing cloud, determined not to let the foundation of her home be wrecked. It was not easy though, to swallow her pain and grief but she didn't want her children to live through a traumatic childhood. She fiercely protected her children and shielded them from bearing the brunt of living with an errant father. She could only do this by donning the dual role of being both father as well as mother at the same time. Naturally, the children grew more and more dependent on her, spending most of their time at home happily in the security of a mother who was always there for them. But her little acts of sacrifice didn't grow unnoticed… it only made them respect her courage and also made them accept their dad with all his imperfections. Anjali was thankful for her two kids who at such a young age were learning to live life with tenacity and resilience… could sense that no one is perfect… no soul is completely black or completely white… there was no doubt that they loved and respected their father, for all his erudition, his love of music, his love for books and his essential goodness. But with a wisdom beyond their years they seemed to comprehend and accept his little weakness too.

For Anjali this indeed was a blessing direct from Heaven and only confirmed her belief in a God who was unfailingly by her side through the rough and tumble of life. For some reason life was indeed giving her a hard bargain, inspite of her being good, inspite of her belief in living a life of service to others, inspite of trying not to hurt or cause any pain to anybody.

But the more she tried to live her life with moral uprightness, the more life seemed to be forcing her to run the gauntlet. And yet she didn't feel totally lost and abandoned. The challenges that she was being made to face seemed to have a higher purpose and she felt heartened and protected in allowing herself to be resigned to Divine will.

Chapter - 8

As challenges kept getting added year after year, Anjali, a book lover as she was, started to plunge herself more and more into reading books of spirituality and mysticism. And the more she plumbed the depths of spirituality the more insights were given to her and the more intuitive she became. It was as if her quest on the spiritual path was a preordained phenomenon and the universe were indeed beckoning her to discover the Unseen… Her yearning to find spiritual moorings led her to the mystical world of yogic masters like Paramahansa Yogananda, Rama Krishna Paramhansa, Dr. Paul Brunton, Ramana Maharshi, Vivekananda, Aurobindo and many of the more contemporary Gurus. All these seers seemed to profess the same truth- the Oneness of the Universe, the one absolute Universal Consciousness centered like the Sun and millions and trillions of souls, like innumerable galaxies following their own spiritual trajectory around it as their individual karma had devised for them to follow… Finally the greatest truth- that all these individual souls, on completion of their journeys would converge in the Universal Soul.

Anjali also knew that everything is out there in the universe- angels, demons, demigods, mysteries, miracles, natural, supernatural, the comprehensible and the incomprehensible… everything is profound, sublime, and in accordance with the working of the Divine Clockwork and whenever the extraordinary did happen sometimes in one's existence, it was to be taken as a Miracle…Miracles abound in everyone's life…all that is needed is receptivity…faith…and acceptance.

She also knew that the world is full of believers as well as sceptics but she would not concern herself with any contradictions. Her heart told her about the existence of the Divine and she was willing to accept it without a shadow of doubt. She knew that she may not attain the level of enlightenment of the spiritual Gurus about whom she read. But she felt happy that in spite of being nowhere near those great, ascended souls in divine awareness yet she had been blessed by a sensitivity that had put her on a spiritual quest, however rudimentary a stage it was in. Whether she would make any progress in that direction she did not worry about. Like Abou Ben Adhem it was enough for her if her name was written by the Angel of light as one who loved her fellow human beings. But all her readings did seem to fortify her from within... over the years she had noticed herself taking everything with equanimity. Her readings, her reflections and her meditations were helping to strengthen her resolve to face challenges boldly... her armour of faith was a defence against any calamity that threatened to strike her. The laws of God are simple – Be good and do good. Everything will be taken care of. Challenges are thrown to us but because He knows their worth. They are the forge in which the soul is shaped...the anvil on which it is hammered... the purgatory through which it comes out perfected...

Chapter - 9

H ER QUEST WHICH LED HER from one spiritual book to another was, unknown to her, preparing her to receive other gifts... the kind of gifts that only heaven can bestow- the gifts of intuition, heightened awareness and the ability to understand that, there was more to the universe than the human mind could comprehend.

She stumbled upon this truth quite unexpectedly. It was when her father had been hospitalized for a serious ailment. With every passing day his chances of making it through, seemed to become slimmer and slimmer. Added to this was the problem of managing a shocked and distraught mother who had somehow fallen into a pit of despair. Seeing her looking shell shocked and benumbed with anxiety, Anjali seemed to lose her own bearings. What words of consolation could she give to her mother when it appeared as if she herself were a bystander watching helplessly as her beloved father was losing his foot hold over the earth. A feeling of gloom pervaded the house as signs and omens... whatever one wished to define them as, started appearing with an ominous certainty. The stopping of three clocks in her parent's house in quick succession, the bursting of tube lights for no apparent reason, the uneasy dreams of accidentally dropping the idols of God or slipping off while climbing stairs, the framed photo of God getting termite-ridden in a house which was spotlessly clean- all these happenings couldn't be dismissed as merely coincidental. The universe was definitely warning them about the impending doom and perhaps even preparing them for something calamitous... Finally the dreaded moment occurred and tearfully they had to bid goodbye to her father, the man who had been the soul of the house for seventy long years!

As surely as they had come, with the death of her father, all the omens and portents stopped abruptly and normalcy was restored. Except for the pain caused due to the bereavement, Anjali felt that the 'bizarre' had left their lives and life had resumed its ordinary pace.

But all was not yet over. A new phenomenon was now occurring in her life. Death had merely ended the mortal life of her father. But the bonds of love couldn't be severed by death… her father returned to them in spirit. At first Anjali assumed that she was probably imagining too much. It couldn't be… The pungent odours of the medicines and the ointments used in the hospital couldn't reappear at home! The strong odours enveloping her couldn't be the figment of a feverish mind. Anjali tried to reason with all the rationale she could apply to understand this strange phenomenon but no, nothing could make her dismiss these strange happenings as hallucinations! Throughout the week till the twelfth day ceremonies she could acutely feel the presence of her father's spirit. Most poignant was the morning of the twelfth day- the day her mother was being bathed by other widows as was the custom prevalent and she was to be divested of her 'mangalsutra' the symbol of her marital status- that day Anjali not only sensed the medicinal odours that assailed her nose and told her that her father's spirit was near, but she distinctly heard a faint whirring noise, just outside the bathroom door as if an invisible wheel were rotating in full speed… she felt a lump form in her throat… clearly, her father's spirit was agitated… He knew how devout his wife had been… how she had prayed to die before her husband…how she had longed to be blessed in this way… With his death she was being made to undergo this intense suffering, a suffering every Indian woman dreads to go through… Anjali could comprehend the suffering both her parents were undergoing. The togetherness of forty years that was snapped in an instant by death and the pangs of separation that they were facing- he in the spirit and she in flesh and blood.

Anjali did all she could to console her mother. But when her mother also began to sense her father's spirit in the house, she drew comfort from the fact that death had not completely severed her ties with her husband and silently, but with a new- found faith, she came to terms with life and learnt to cope with her predicament. Mother and daughter kept this fact to themselves. There was no point in sharing such information with others who were likely to scoff at the idea or consider them crazy. It was enough to know that somehow his spirit was still around them and would take care of them. It was only for a few months that they had sensed his unseen presence, on and off... but it was enough to strengthen them and affirm their belief that soul connections are an undeniable fact of existence.

But if her father had shown such reluctance initially about accepting his death, her mother, when she died ten years after his death, departed as if she had been ready and waiting for it. Anjali recollected that three months before her demise, she had shown signs of deteriorating health, with kidney malfunction, being the main cause. But as the end approached, unknown to Anjali, she had made her preparations. With the gift given to the pious few of precognition, she even chose the date of her demise. Two days before 'Maha Sivarathri' one of the most auspicious days in the Hindu Calendar, she complained of sickness and rang up Anjali who had gone to Hyderabad for some personal work.

"Come soon dear, don't be late," she whispered to Anjali on the phone.

Anjali could not help detect the mild anxiety in her mother's tone and tried to reassure her lovingly.

"Don't worry mummy, I'll be with you by tomorrow evening."

When Anjali reached her mother's house, she found her mother looking weak but not as sick looking as she had feared. The evening was spent in an exchange of a lot of love and tenderness... Anjali's mother pulled her daughter close to her... Anjali felt the thin, shrunk frame of her mother and felt the first stirrings of fear. The moment every daughter dreads to face seemed to be inching close with every passing moment…her mother meant many things to her —security, experience, support, guidance, wise counsel… What if?… Anjali's heart was turning cold with a nameless dread. By midnight her health deteriorated further and she had to be moved to hospital. Anjali remembered how Anand had taken utmost care of his mother-in-law. Trust him, to rise to the occasion… Why couldn't he always be just as responsible and caring? Anjali thought, feeling secretly happy and proud that by attending to her mother he was also receiving the blessing of this ailing woman.

The next night passed on in the hospital cabin. Anjali felt closer to her mother than ever before. When her mother soiled the bedsheet in the thick of the night and no hospital attendant was available, Anjali lovingly cleaned her mother, treating her as if she were her own child. Her mother seemed to be in a mild state of delirium. Anjali kept a constant vigil on her. She looked deeply at the shrunk frame, the tiny feet, the gnarled fingers and the pale sweet face as if to print the memory of her mother and these moments into the core of her heart. She held her mother's hand and sat by her bedside the whole night.

Once when she found herself dozing in the early hours of the morning, she was awakened by the soft voice of her mother, "take some rest dear…"

Anjali felt a stab of pain in her heart. Concern for her child even now… even when she was so ill. She hugged her mother and shed silent tears…

As it was Maha Sivarathi day, she went home to do her Pooja leaving her brother Shridhar, to watch over her, while the doctors ministered to her. Anjali had barely reached home when her brother called to relay the sad news of their mother's demise.

She was plunged into grief. This was totally a rude shock. Her mother couldn't go off just like that! She was sick no doubt but not so much as to leave so suddenly. When she saw her mother's body she understood what might have happened. By her own choice, very much like the 'samadhi' taken by saints, her mother had taken leave of this world. She was dumb founded to see the look of rapture in the serene face and the sense of surrender writ large in the lifeless eyes that were staring heavenwards...

What a day the lady had chosen to die in... the most auspicious of days... that could have been earned only through life times of good karma. And unlike her father who had been reluctant to leave this world and who could not sever his ties with his loved ones, there was no such trace in her mother's departure. It was as if her mother's only longing had been to go back to her real home...the home of the Divine Father. Anjali detected no signs of any spirit presence ever in the house.

The vacuum that Anjali felt after her mother's demise took a long time to be filled... but it strengthened her spiritual moorings. In the last few months of her life, a dramatic change had occurred in her mother's demeanor. She had become more and more withdrawn, reflective and silent. This change had been so gradual as to be almost unnoticeable but it had not been missed by Anjali. Reflecting on the matter, post her mother's demise, Anjali could understand that her mother had indeed been provided an insight or revelation that had made her lose interest in the material world and turn to the world of spirit. But it was probably too profound an experience and much too personal to be shared with anybody...Anjali was sure that her parents were reunited and this thought offered some consolation and helped her to tide over her sorrow.

Chapter - 10

EVERY STORY USUALLY HAS A villain…the character who adds a twist to the plot… the person who affirms the belief that life does not always sail on an even keel… the ship of life gets caught in the fiercest of storms and is thrown about, tossed about, is made to ride over dangerous crests and the crew are severely tested. But just as a ship cannot be expected to proceed without braving such storms, life cannot be lived through without such people appearing now and then. Like a storm they come, catching us unawares and wreaking havoc in our lives.

Anjali and her husband were facing one of the most difficult times in their life. Anand had come home one evening from the hospital looking worried and dejected. His face looked dark and the creases on his forehead stood out prominently.

"I have bad news,' Anjali noticed the small voice with which he had spoken. "I am in a problem. Someone has registered a complaint against me. I don't know what actually it is about but…"

To Anjali the words had sounded like, a thunderclap. "Why! What are you saying? Complaint! but why?" she exclaimed, her heart beating hard.

"After seeing the patients, I went to the doctor's rest room to smoke and just then some high official came in on an inspection. Not finding me in the clinic he made a surprise entry into the rest room, found me smoking and went back. This happened two days ago but today I received the official order accusing me of being drunk at work. I tried to explain that I was not drunk, that I had actually seen twenty patients, which can be confirmed by seeing the entries in the patient register, and that I had merely smoked a cigarette in the adjoining rest room to relax... but to no avail. The order has been issued. Till an enquiry is conducted I cannot go back to the hospital," he said quietly.

Anjali started crying... the tears just refused to stop flowing down... How terrible! A multitude of thoughts attacked her all at once. What would her relatives and friends think! How would they manage running the house without money! Neel's tuition fees, hostel fees, the day to day expenses... how was she to run the house... How long before the enquiry was conducted and Anand could be given a clearance?

Why? God! Why? She cried, unable to comprehend this terrible twist in her life. After putting up so much with Anand's drinking and trying to put on a brave front in spite of all that she was suffering, it seemed unfair that life hadn't quite finished with her... what had she done to deserve this fate!

And as if the blows that fate seemed to be dealing out to her weren't enough, one day, Anjali came home to find their car smashed badly on the left side, one headlight completely broken. She went into the house, took one look at her husband and understood what might have happened. Because of his condition, he must have hit the light pole...of late she had seen him looking more and more depressed...his drinking had also increased as a result...in his inebriated condition he had probably not been able to park the car properly and hit the electricity pole.

When she made a call for the mechanic she had literally made a call to the devil! That was when Prabhu, a mechanic she had never seen before, walked into her house and into their lives. In no time, he got the car repaired and won not only their appreciation but also their trust. To Anjali the defenceless woman that she was... the blade of grass that she had been turned into, crushed under the feet of a merciless fate, Prabhu came in as a ray of hope into their dark lives. With every passing day he got closer and closer to them. He soon became a friend and confidante for everybody in the family.

He became a veritable 'Genie of the lamp.' Any work that had to be attended to, whether it was shopping for provisions, post office work, bank work or visits to the temple- he was unfailingly there. The family started depending entirely on him. He became a sort of 'brother' to Anjali, uncle to her children and a personal aide to Anand. It was but natural that he would report every morning at their house and give 'company' to Anand who was sitting idle at home, as the complaint against him was still in the process of being investigated.

With only the subsistence pay coming home as Anand's salary, they ran the gauntlet trying to tide over the financial crisis and in no time she had to use her gold to take loans from the bank to manage heavier expenses like college fees, etc.

'Akka (elder sister) don't worry. I am there for you people. I think God sent me just to help you people out. I know many people whose cars I have repaired. So if loans have to be taken or for, any other help, you can safely trust me. With such smooth talking, he gained the family's trust. Nobody could really blame them. Considering the dire straits they were in, one couldn't blame them for looking up to him as a God- sent angel. Gradually the trust became so great that he started using their money liberally for all the odd jobs that he was entrusted with. And never felt the need to show any bills. Anjali and Anand also stopped asking for the bills as he was doing many chores for them like a family member and a sense of obligation for all the support he was giving rendered them mute.

They didn't realize that they were being cheated of a lot of money till quite some time had passed. But in all that period a lot of damage had already been done. In the name of giving 'company' to Anand, Prabhu regularly started bringing liquor home to him. When Anjali accosted him one day, his suave reply was, 'isn't it better that I bring him a limited quantity every day, rather than that he goes out and probably knocks down a man or two. Drunken driving is severely punishable and killing or injuring somebody while high on booze is a non- bailable offence. And what if he himself is hurt in an accident. Do you realise how terrible your life would be?"

Anjali would be frightened to silence after listening to this. But as fate would have it everything turned against her. There seemed to be no end to the problems that besieged her. Prabhu's entry into their lives, his getting them to be totally dependent on him, and her husband's increased addiction to drinking- nothing was going right... she felt as if being dragged into a bog of misfortune...But gradually they realised that Prabhu was a fox in the garb of an angel.

When they were reeling under the pressure of such severe trials, as a further test of her strength, her son got involved in a major accident for no fault of his. A call from his college in New Delhi one evening sent the family into a spin. "Madam, I am Professor Jha calling from your son's college. Neel was hit by a drunk motor cyclist and he is admitted in the hospital. He is conscious but there is a bad fracture in his right leg. We are taking care of him but please start immediately...He is undergoing an emergency operation tonight. But he will be required to undergo the main surgery only after a few days."

For a family already going through near penury, the news was nothing short of calamitous! Her darling son, her son who was such a good dancer, basketball player, football player, so active and energetic, now lying injured grievously. Anjali couldn't bear it. The wheel of misfortune seemed to be turning over and over, flattening out their lives, snuffing out the little breath that was left in them. But the moment had to be lived through. The operations had to be done to put the boy back on his feet. More gold had to be put into the bank and further loans incurred...

It became all the more difficult since Anjali seemed to be shouldering everything herself. She didn't wish to cause any pain to her aged parents-in –law and kept everything concealed from them. She, however, told them about Neel's accident as she and her husband were rushing to New Delhi for the operation and they didn't know how long it would be before they could return. And she also had to leave her daughter behind as she was still at school and couldn't be made to miss her school. Leaving her in the care of kindly neighbours the couple rushed to New Delhi.

After that everything went about with mechanical precision- the operations, bringing her son back, having him at home as a patient for three months before he got back to his hostel, the period of intense testing as loans and more loans had to be incurred. Money took up precedence over everything. Her first waking thought was about money and she went to bed with one calculation or another preoccupying her mind.

But with patience and fortitude and her staunch faith in God, Anjali saw her family through the crises. The silver lining appeared with the charges against her husband being dropped after a couple of enquires. Her son regained his health and managed to bag a good internship at a reputed organisation at Delhi, in his final semester and her daughter completed her twelfth successfully and gained admission into a good college for graduate studies.

As for Prabhu the family could finally see through his veneer of goodness and shut him out of their lives after directly confronting him with the truth. They also realised the high price they had had to pay as a result of trusting the devil. They had no idea how much money they had lost out to him and there was some gold too that the fellow had cleverly manipulated out of their hands. But they decided to lodge no complaint with the police because they didn't have a single proof against him and they didn't want to compound their problems, knowing the kind of trickster he was. She believed in Divine justice and in the inexorable laws of Karma. *What goes around comes back...* She knew that one day Prabhu would have to answer for his own misdeeds.

Therefore Anjali sought no further redressal for the wrong that had happened in her life. Her only thought was of gratitude to God who, though he had appeared distant at times, had always been there throughout the period of intense testing. Feeling grateful to God in the face of gruelling challenges was no easy matter. But the tenacity to withstand them came from a dogged faith in the Almighty. Behind every problem there is an inner cause. Life is a juxtaposition of opposites- 'Good' and 'bad', 'ugly' and 'beautiful', 'joy' and 'sorrow' and even 'simple' and 'complicated'. While it is filled with innocent and happy moments like a joyous birdsong, the gentle swaying of a leaf in the breeze or the gurgling of the lucid waters of a brook, it also consists of grim subjects like sin, sickness, suffering and death. Between these two extremes man lives out his life and the best way he can do this is by living it as graciously and peacefully as he can. Life also has a pattern to its flow. Just as day follows night and so on, once sorrow comes, joy is sure to follow... So instead of questioning the why and wherefore of a problem, Anjali saw it as the cyclic pattern, typical of life. Who is spared of suffering and trials? Everyone has to go through this cycle. And why give up in despair. If we count our blessings we will find that we have less to complain of than scores of other people who have problems of a greater magnitude. Troubles to Anjali didn't mean the absence of God. They actually meant that God was near and he was carrying her through the crises...

Chapter - 11

CRISES! THE WORD CRISES BROUGHT a fresh lump to Anjali's throat. Her eyes smarted with unshed tears. What greater crises than the loss of a husband! The recent two months once again flashed through her mind. Her husband's deteriorating health, his stubborn refusal to be admitted to hospital for fear of being deprived of his 'bottle', the way he had to be forcibly admitted, his being rushed to the I.C.U, the tense moments thereafter, as he wavered between life and death and the final moment when he passed on, leaving them all dazed and shattered. Anjali remembered how her heart seemed to turn into a stone... how mechanically she had seen through all the arrangements for the funeral and the rituals that followed. The first thought that came to her mind as she saw her husband being laid out on the bier was that of resignation.

'His fight with the demons of 'drinking' and 'smoking' is finally over. He has lost his life to them but he is finally rid of them and must be at peace,' she thought sadly. She missed him terribly but saw a new meaning in his death. She saw the end of a good but weak-willed man. She saw the way he had been tormented by his own habits. His struggle to overcome his weaknesses and his final surrender to them...

There was a peaceful pallor on his face. Now at last the long fight was finally over. He was at peace with his soul. Anjali remembered the countless arguments they had had over his addiction which had robbed him of all his intelligence, and erudition, had robbed him of his gifts like his taste for music, and books, his talent at cooking and chiefly, above all else, the great doctor he had been, blessed with that healing touch few people have. People thronged to his funeral. Everyone had one reason or the other to attend it. They either remembered his nobility or his great wit or, as a patient said tearfully, "For me, it is to bemoan the loss of a life that could have served people for many more years, if the devil had spared him. He was a good doctor as well as a good human being Madam."

After that, the months had followed with a mechanical progression. The suddenness of his death left Anjali feeling dazed and confused. This was a new feeling... she was now a *widow*! How was she to live the rest of her life... so many unfulfilled responsibilities ... his aged parents... Her two children...

She didn't blame God. What could God do if Anand had wantonly destroyed himself. God gives us the free will to make a choice. Anand had chosen death over life. Even if it was his 'karma' there would still have been a way out if he had turned to God instead of giving the reins to the devil... Still it was a kind God who had spared him unnecessary physical suffering, for had he even survived the ordeal, the months of recovery would have been long and painful. The doctors had not minced their words. Anand's condition was so bad that even if by a miracle he had survived, the recovery would have been long and arduous and he would have suffered.

'Veera patni, Veera Mata' (warrior wife, warrior mother) Anjali remembered how often her husband had used these words to praise her when she had taken on the responsibility of running the household as he had gradually withdrawn himself from day to day chores.

Today, after his demise, she remembered these words and the expression of love and pride she had seen in his eyes as he used to utter them.

'Yes dear, you have indeed forced me to become a warrior woman. Perhaps you had foreseen all this beforehand and prepared me for this day...' Anjali mused sadly.

For the first time she felt the ripples of fear. The enormity of the responsibilities that lay before her stuck her with a force that led her to break into great sobs. She had wept inconsolably... felt miserable and alone, like a boat adrift on an ocean... but through her pain and loneliness emerged a new feeling of strength. Through the disharmony of chaotic thoughts emerged the peaceful music of God's love. Somehow, it was then that God began to speak to her... in the wee hours of the morning when her eyes would fly open with fear and she would miss her husband and cry, it was then that she felt the hand of God upon her... she would walk into the balcony and gaze at the still starry night, picturing her husband somewhere among the stars overhead, and she would feel the nearness of God very acutely. The gentle morning breeze, the sacred silence, the crispness of the air, the twitter of the birds- this was the way God spoke to her...this was the way he reassured her...such a beautiful orchestration of moments, such perfect harmony in nature was inconceivable without a maestro at work... He is the conductor who orchestrates the rhythms of everybody's lives...It was those early morning meditations that slowly but surely strengthened her.

Epilogue

"MA'AM PLEASE, FASTEN YOUR SEAT belt," the polite voice of the cabin crew broke into her reveries.

They were to land soon in Dubai. Anjali could see the flurry of activity as people were donning their seat belts.

She peered out of her window. The blue of the skies contrasted with the landscape below. Stretches and stretches of yellow sand that glistened in the morning sunlight. As the plane flew further, she could make out the rows and rows of beautiful buildings standing tall like packs of cards… It took another two hours before she finally wheeled her baggage out of the exit doors of the airport to the waiting cab. Her friend Shweta had sent the office car to pick her up. She looked forward to meeting her friend who had arranged this new job for her.

As the taxi sped along the smooth, polished roads, Anjali found herself thinking again. The manner in which this job had come her way, so soon after the tragedy in her life, seemed like a part of a divine plan. God was directing her life, filling up some moments with sorrow, some moments with joy, some with surprises. It was his way of carrying her through crises. He had allowed demons to come and angels as well… the demons had thrown challenges in her face… the angels had helped her affirm her faith in God… her friends Indira and Elisha who had introduced Jesus into her life… Anagha who had shown her the peacefulness that lay in Buddhist tenets… her mother who had shown her the joy in immersing oneself in Krishna consciousness… her guru who had revealed to her the powers of Goddess Shakti. Anjali did not concern herself with names. She only listened to the core of her heart… that was where her God was. That was where she directed her prayers and that was where she got her answers from. Now that God was showing her a new life. She felt no fear. God was her anchor and her saviour.

Anjali also remembered again how a strange wish, made on a dark night when she had been sitting on a swing and watching airplanes fly overhead, had been fulfilled… The magical is not something that happened in the heavens… it is very much a part of our everyday lives… we live in the midst of miracles…

She had indeed boarded an International Flight and reached Dubai! Not, as she had assumed going with her children in some distant future, but so soon and by dint of her own talent, a friends kindness and God's infinite grace.

Anjali remembered her parents who, alas, were not alive to see this achievement. But she knew they were watching from above and blessing her.

And there remained *one little wish*, yet to be fulfilled…

Anjali remembered the words of her husband as he had often goaded her, "Write something every day. You have that talent in you to become a writer. Write something, even if it is about the way I trouble you. Describe your experience, relive it through your words. Your experiences with your children at school, with Neel and Nitya. Write something… anything… every day. Don't worry about being published. Just write for that pure joy of writing…"

Anjali felt tears trickle down her face as she recollected the earnest look in his eyes as he had entreated her again and again to take to writing.

'Yes dear, someday I will…someday I will write a book about us…' She promised to herself silently. As the cab sped along the busy roads of Dubai she sat back, preparing herself for the new life ahead… a new page was being opened in the book of her life. The past was already behind her. The future was beckoning her like a fresh green pasture…she remembered her children with a sense of pride. How brave they had been…what resilience they had shown…they had had to bear the loss of one parent through death and another through distance…yet it was they who had encouraged her to take up this new opportunity…

"Don't worry about us mother. We will be fine. Don't lose this wonderful opportunity. I will take care of Nitya and Reggie." Neel had reassured her, already sounding very mature.

"Yes, mamma, we will be alright. If God is showing you a new path you must take it. He wants you to teach other children. He wants you to go global," Nitya had said good –humouredly.

Anjali sat back, gazing out of the window of the cab at the polished and sparkling vistas of the land which was to be her new home, wondering about all the new people who would enter the pages of her life and the new challenges that would come her way…but assured that there was a *friend* who was unfailingly by her side, through the peaks and troughs of life.

****

Printed in the United States
By Bookmasters